The NeveR GiRls

the
space
between

WRitten by
kiki Thorpe

Illustrated by
Jana Christy

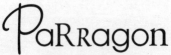

PaRragon

Bath · New York · Cologne · Melbourne · Delhi
Hong Kong · Shenzhen · Singapore · Amsterdam

This edition published by Parragon Books Ltd in 2014

Parragon Books Ltd
Chartist House
15–17 Trim Street
Bath BA1 1HA, UK
www.parragon.com

ISBN 978-1-4723-0842-9

Printed in UK

Never Land

Far away from the world we know, on the distant seas of dreams, lies an island called Never Land. It is a place full of magic, where mermaids sing, fairies play and children never grow up. Adventures happen every day, and anything is possible.

There are two ways to reach Never Land. One is to find the island yourself. The other is for it to find you. Finding Never Land on your own takes a lot of luck and a pinch of fairy dust. Even then, you will only find the island if it wants to be found.

Every once in a while, Never Land drifts close to our world ... so close, a fairy's laugh slips through. And every once in an even longer while, Never Land opens its doors to a special few. Believing in magic and fairies from the bottom of your heart can make the extraordinary happen. If you suddenly hear tiny bells or feel a sea breeze where there is no sea, pay careful attention. Never Land may be nearby. You could find yourself there in a blink of an eye.

Torth Mountain

Pixie Hollow

SKULL ROCK

Mermaid Lagoon

One day, four special girls came to Never Land
in just this way. This is their story.

Chapter 1

Lainey Winters was soaring.

For a brief moment, her heart seemed to stop. The ground fell away, and she rose up, up, up … and over the fallen log.

An instant later, she touched down again, bounding through the forest on the back of a doe. Trees flashed by in a blur of green. Lainey dug her hands deeper into the doe's fur. She held on tight as they darted round bushes and flew over stones.

Leaves crashed above. Lainey looked up and saw a squirrel racing through the trees. A tiny fairy sat on its back, her long brown plait swinging behind her. The squirrel leaped from branch to branch, keeping pace with the doe.

Lainey leaned forward, urging her doe on. The fairy did the same.

Ahead was a small clearing. In its centre stood a tall maple tree, bigger than any other tree in the forest. From a distance, its branches seemed to sparkle and move. This was due to the many fairies who hummed around it like bees around a honeycomb. The maple was called the Home Tree, and it was the heart of Pixie Hollow, the Never fairies' world.

Lainey steered the doe towards the Home Tree. Even without looking up,

she could sense the fairy on the squirrel following above her.

A few feet from the tree, the squirrel shot past Lainey. It landed on a branch and came to a stop just as Lainey and the doe pulled up at the Home Tree's roots.

Lainey laughed. "You beat me again, Fawn!" she called to the fairy on the squirrel.

"I wouldn't be much of an animal-talent fairy if I couldn't win a race against a Clumsy, would I?" Fawn replied, smiling.

Lainey slid off the doe's back, pushing the big glasses she wore up her nose. She didn't care about winning or losing. For her, the joy was in riding the deer, feeling it turn when she wanted to turn, knowing when it would leap.

In her real life, the one where she went to school and lived with her parents, Lainey had never even had a pet, not so much as a goldfish. But here in Never Land, she'd played hide-and-seek with wild hares. She'd listened to birdsong. She'd cradled baby hedgehogs in her hands. Things she'd never dreamed possible seemed to happen every day here.

As Lainey patted the deer's back, Fawn flew down and landed on its head. She whispered something in the doe's ear. The doe ducked its head once, as if nodding. Then it turned and bounded away into the forest.

"What did you say?" Lainey asked.

"I told her next time I'd ride with her, and you could ride the squirrel," Fawn joked.

"I want to learn to do that," Lainey said.

Fawn raised her eyebrows. "Ride a squirrel? Don't you think you're a bit too big?"

Lainey giggled. "No, I want to learn how to speak Deer."

"You have to wriggle before you can hop," Fawn replied.

"I have to do what?" asked Lainey, confused.

"It's an animal-fairy saying," Fawn explained. "It means you have to start slowly. Talking to deer is tricky. They can be pretty snooty about accents. Let's hear how your Mouse is coming along."

Furrowing her brow, Lainey squeaked, *"Eeee-eee!"*

Fawn had been teaching Lainey how to speak the language of mice.

So far, Lainey had only learned one squeak. Loosely translated, it meant "Are your whiskers well?"

Two dairy mice that were sniffing around nearby lifted their heads to look at Lainey.

"Not bad," said Fawn, nodding. "Now let's hear you call that chickadee." She pointed to a plump little bird sitting on a branch.

"But I don't know Chickadee!" Lainey protested.

"It's easy," said Fawn. "Just go like this." Pursing her lips, Fawn let out a whistle that sounded like *tseedle dee tseedle dee deet.* "You try."

Lainey did her best to copy Fawn.

She pursed her lips and whistled. But all that came out was a sad *feewp*!

To her surprise, the chickadee flew over and landed on her finger.

"How did I do that?" Lainey asked. Then she noticed Fawn laughing. "Wait a second. *You* called him over, didn't you?"

"So what if I did?" Fawn said with an impish grin. "He wouldn't have come if he didn't want to. Animals like you, Lainey. I'd say you're becoming a real animal-talent Clumsy."

Lainey blushed.

Fawn pulled a sunflower seed from her pocket. She held it out to the chickadee, who took it in his beak and flew away.

"Well, I'm hungry," Fawn said. "Want to see what the baking-talent fairies have whipped up today?"

Lainey shook her head. "I'm going to find the other girls. See you later?"

"Sure," said Fawn. "I think there's a nest of robin's eggs that need a hand with hatching. Maybe you can help me." With a wave, she flew off.

Lainey started across the meadow, her spirits high. Fawn's compliment still rang in her ears. *A real animal-talent Clumsy.* Lainey couldn't help smiling every time she thought about it.

Maybe it's true, Lainey thought. *Maybe I really do have animal talent.*

Before coming to Pixie Hollow, Lainey had never felt particularly special. She wasn't beautiful like her friend Mia, or brave like her friend Kate. She wasn't good at sports and she didn't get the best grades in school. In fact, Lainey hadn't been sure she was good at anything at all.

But that had changed when she'd started spending time with the animal-talent fairies. Lainey was learning how to listen to animals and how to watch them. And she had a knack for it!

A real animal-talent Clumsy.

A rustling noise above her made Lainey look up. She paused to watch a flock of flamingos pass. She loved seeing the pale pink birds against the brilliant blue of the sky. The flamingos had been one of the very first creatures she'd seen in Never Land, and she never tired of watching them.

Lainey continued across the meadow and made her way to Havendish Stream. There she found Kate, Mia and Gabby, the friends

who had come to Never Land with her.
They were sailing boats with the water-
talent fairies. Tiny fairies in red, gold
and green leaf-boats drifted around on
the current while the girls blew wind
into their sails.

The freckled, curly-haired fairy named Prilla was there, too. Prilla was the reason the girls had come to Never Land. She had a talent unlike any other in Pixie Hollow. She could travel to the world of humans and back again just by blinking. One day, she'd travelled to Mia and Gabby's back garden and accidentally brought the four girls back to Pixie Hollow with her.

But Prilla had discovered that she couldn't blink the girls back home, so the fairies of Pixie Hollow had taken them in. That had been days ago – or was it weeks? Lainey wasn't sure. Time passed strangely in Never Land, where every day was sunny and no one ever grew up or grew old.

"Hi, Lainey," Mia said. "Where have you been?"

"I was riding in the woods with Fawn," Lainey said.

Kate stood, brushing off the knees of her jeans. "We're thinking about going to Skull Rock, just to see what it's like," she told Lainey. Kate had made it her mission to explore every corner of Never Land.

"Prilla says we might see a mermaid there!" Gabby chimed in excitedly. Gabby was only five, but she was every bit as adventurous as the other girls.

"We're not going for long," Mia added. "There's a fairy dance tonight, and I want to make sure we're back in time. The weaving-talent fairies are going to plait jasmine into my hair!"

"Want to come?" Kate asked Lainey.

Lainey hesitated. She wanted to go with her friends, but she also wanted to watch chicks hatching with Fawn. There were so many fun things happening in Never Land. Sometimes it was hard to decide what to do first.

Just then, they spotted a fairy flying towards them. As she came closer, the girls saw it was Skye. The fairy's rose-petal cap was crooked on her head, and she seemed to be out of breath.

"I've been looking all over for you girls!" she said with a gasp. "It's time!"

"Time for what?" asked Kate.

"Never Land is on the move again," Skye replied.

The girls looked at each other in dismay. They knew what that meant.

It was time for them to go home.

Chapter 2

Skye, the seeing-talent fairy, was the one who had figured out how the girls had come to Never Land. She'd also figured out why they couldn't return home again.

As Skye had explained it, Never Land was unlike other islands. It drifted on the seas of children's dreams, moving wherever it wished. One day, it had drifted close to the world of Clumsies, so close that the tiniest bit of magic had pulled the four unsuspecting girls to its shores. Kate, Mia, Lainey and Gabby had always believed in fairies, but their wildest dreams came true when they had arrived there on Prilla's blink.

Then the island had drifted away again – and the four girls had been stranded.

But now Never Land was close to the girls' world again. "I saw the mainland with my own eyes," Skye told the girls. "Prilla can blink you back home again – right away! But you must hurry!"

"But what about Skull Rock?" said Kate.

"And the mermaid?" said Gabby.

"And the fairy dance?" said Mia.

"And the robin chicks?" said Lainey.

"If you don't go now, you might not make it back. Who knows when Never Land will be this close to your world again?" Skye said.

The girls had always known this day would come. They just hadn't thought it would come so soon. Not one of them wanted to leave, but if they didn't, they might never see their families again.

So they would have to say goodbye – to the flower-filled meadow and burbling Havendish Stream, to the magnificent Home Tree and all the kind, lovely fairies who lived there. *And it isn't just a 'see-you-later' goodbye,* Lainey thought. *It is really and truly farewell.* Children who left Never Land never came back, the fairy Tinker Bell had told them. They grew up too quickly and forgot about it.

With heavy hearts, the four girls went to their willow-tree room to pack.

Sunlight shone through the willow's branches as they entered, casting a jade-green glow over the room. Lainey looked at the hammocks where they'd slept, the firefly lanterns hanging from the tree limbs and the moss carpet on the ground.

"There isn't anything to pack," she realized. They'd come to Pixie Hollow with nothing but the clothes they had on.

"I want to take *something* home with me," Mia said. She picked up a tiny folding fan that a fairy had left behind. The fan was made from daisy petals held together with pine needles.

Mia put it in her pocket.

Kate found an itty-bitty kaleidoscope that a pots-and-pans fairy had cobbled together from bits of scrap metal. A water-talent fairy had cast the lens from a single drop of dew.

Gabby chose a daisy garland that the garden-talent fairies had woven. She placed it on her head like a crown.

"It'll wilt, you know," Mia warned her little sister.

"I don't care," Gabby said, sticking out her lip.

Lainey looked around for a souvenir of her own. She considered her liquorice-twig toothbrush or one of the firefly lanterns, but neither seemed right. She wished she could take a pet home with her – her doe, maybe, or one of the livelier squirrels. But of course she knew the animals belonged in Never Land. Besides, her mother would never allow it – she didn't even like goldfish.

At last she picked up a mouse-herder's lasso. It was made of plaited Never grass. Lainey slipped it over her wrist like a bracelet, pulling the end tight. She remembered the day Fawn had used it to lasso a wayward dairy mouse.

Thinking of that reminded Lainey of her lesson earlier that day. *I'll never learn how to speak Deer now.*

The thought filled Lainey with sadness.

Prilla appeared in the doorway of the willow room. Her bright, open face was unusually glum. "Skye says you must hurry. There isn't much time."

Taking one last look around their room, the girls followed Prilla out of the door.

Beneath a hawthorn tree on the far side of Pixie Hollow was a ring of mushrooms. This was the fairy circle, where Pixie Hollow's magic was strongest.

When Lainey and her friends got there, they were surprised to see all the fairies gathered together. Animal fairies, fast-flying fairies, water fairies, light fairies, garden fairies, harvest fairies, baking fairies, dressmaking fairies, art fairies, storytelling fairies and dozens more. Fairies of every talent had come to see the girls off.

Clarion, queen of the Never fairies, stood at the head of the fairy circle. Her wings were folded solemnly behind her to mark the sad moment. She nodded to the girls to step inside the circle.

"The fairies have a parting gift for you," the queen said. At her cue, Terence, a dust-talent sparrow man, flew forward. He held out a velvet sack no bigger than a peach stone.

"It's a bit of fairy dust," the queen explained. "Just one pinch for each of you. Perhaps one day you can use it to find your way back to Pixie Hollow."

"How will we know the way?" Kate wondered. "Is there a map?"

The queen spread her hands. "I can't say for sure. Never Land drifts about on the waves, always moving. But some say

that to get here from the mainland you should look for the Second Star to the Right and fly straight on till morning."

Thanking the queen, Kate took the bag of dust from Terence and put it in her pocket.

Several fairies and sparrow men came forward then to say special goodbyes to the girls. Lainey searched the crowd for Fawn, but she couldn't see her friend anywhere.

At last, Skye entered the circle. "You must go now," she told Prilla and the girls. "Never Land is on the move again. Soon it will be too late."

Kate, Lainey, Mia and Gabby held hands. Prilla landed in Gabby's open palm.

"Fly sa-" the queen started to say as Prilla blinked.

In that moment, all of Pixie Hollow winked out. The trees, the flowers, the sky, the fairy circle and the fairies themselves – everything vanished. The rest of Queen Clarion's words were lost.

*

An instant later, the girls found themselves in Mia and Gabby's back garden. They looked around at the tall wooden fence, the neatly mowed lawn and the tidy rows of petunias in the flower bed.

A ball sat nearby in the grass. Lainey picked it up, turning it over in her hands. They'd been playing a game with the ball just before they had blinked to Never Land. That seemed like a lifetime ago. Like something she'd dreamed.

"Are we really home?" asked Gabby.

Kate pinched herself. "I think so," she said, but she didn't sound certain.

They heard a high bell-like noise, like the tinkle of a fairy's laugh. All the girls turned towards the sound, but it was only Mia's cat, Bingo. The bells on Bingo's collar jingled as he ran towards them.

Mia scooped the cat up in her arms. She buried her face in his fur. "Oh, Bingo! I missed you!"

"*Meow*," Bingo complained as Mia squeezed him tightly. He wriggled out of her arms and wandered off to chase grasshoppers.

Just then, the back door to the house opened. "Gabby, are you out here?" called a familiar voice.

"Mami!" Gabby squealed. She went running towards her mother, her curls bouncing and her fairy wings flapping on her back.

Mia turned to Lainey and Kate with wide eyes. "What am I going to tell her?" she whispered. "We've been gone for *days*!"

"Remember what Prilla taught us about a blink," Lainey reminded her. "When she travels on a blink, time moves differently."

Kate looked worried. "Let's hope it's true. Otherwise, we're all going to be in for it."

"Do you think it'd be the same if we fly to Never Land?" Lainey wondered. "Does time stop the same way?"

"Speaking of that," Mia said, "what about the fairy dust? Shouldn't we put it somewhere safe?"

"It's very safe. I've got it right here," Kate said, patting her pocket.

An odd look flashed across her face. Kate dug her hand into her pocket. Then she checked her other pocket. She turned both pockets inside out.

Mia frowned. "Kate, that's not funny. Quit messing around."

"I'm not joking," Kate said in a choked voice. "The fairy dust – it's gone!"

Chapter 3

Fawn sat alone in the Home Tree courtyard, twirling the end of her plait between her fingers. Lainey, Mia, Kate and Gabby had gone to the fairy circle – any moment now, they'd be on their way back to their real homes. Fawn knew she should see them off. But she couldn't bring herself to go.

Fawn hated goodbyes. As a Never fairy, she rarely had to say them. Fairies hardly ever left Pixie Hollow, and when they did it was never for long. As for her animal friends, Fawn could see them whenever she wanted, because the creatures of Never Land never grew old.

But now her new Clumsy friends were gone, and she hadn't said so much as 'fly safely'. Not even to Lainey, whom Fawn liked especially. Fawn felt tears pricking her eyes.

"You knew this day would come," she scolded herself. "There's no sense crying over it."

At last, Fawn got to her feet. But instead of flying to the fairy circle, she flew in the opposite direction towards the dairy barn. When Fawn's spirits were low, she liked to visit the dairy mice. She was always happiest around animals.

As Fawn pulled open the heavy door, the mice lifted their heads in greeting.

"How are you, Thistledown? Feeling well, Cloverseed?" she asked as she walked among them. The mice came forward to snuffle her pockets, the bells round their necks chiming faintly. Fawn scratched them behind their ears.

"Where's Milkweed?" she wondered, noticing an empty stall.

The mice only blinked in reply. Fawn understood mice well enough to know that not one of them had noticed Milkweed was missing until now. Mice could be self-centred that way.

"I reckon he's wandered off," she said. "Probably raiding Rosetta's garden for seeds again." Milkweed was a good name for the missing mouse because, like a weed, he was always turning up where he wasn't wanted. "I'll have to go and find him."

Fawn was glad to have something to do to take her mind off the girls. Leaving the dairy barn, she headed outside, calling for Milkweed in soft squeaks. "Milkweed! Where are you, you little fur ball?"

Fawn looked in Rosetta's garden, but she didn't see Milkweed there. She tried other gardens, then circled Pixie Hollow, flying in wider and wider loops.

When she came to Havendish Stream, she paused. Beyond was the great forest of Never Land. Fawn didn't think the little mouse could have crossed the stream on his own.

She was about to turn back when her eyes fell on the stream bank. There in the mud, clear as day, was a mouse's paw print.

Fawn sighed. "Oh, bugs and beetles. What are you up to now, Milkweed?"

She flew across the stream and came to a stop in front of a massive fig tree. It was so large that it looked like several trees grown together. At the base of the tree was a hollow she had never noticed before. To Fawn, the hole seemed as big as a cave.

Were Fawn's ears playing tricks on her or did she hear a bell? She listened carefully. Yes, there it was – a faint jingling. It seemed to be coming from inside the fig tree.

She peered cautiously into the hollow. Fawn wasn't afraid of most animals. She'd talked her way out of tight spots with snakes, badgers and even an owl. Still, she wasn't foolish enough to walk blindly into a predator's nest.

"Helloooooo?" Fawn called into the darkness. Silence greeted her.

Taking a deep breath, Fawn flew into the tree.

Like all fairies, Fawn glowed. But her glow only allowed her to see a couple of inches in front of her. She flew slowly, shivering as she brushed against cobwebs.

Fawn could no longer hear the bell. "Milkweed?" she called.

Just then, Fawn saw light ahead. But how could that be? Wasn't the mouth of the hollow behind her? Had she turned round? *Fawn, you doodlehead,* she said to herself. *You've been flying in a circle!*

If Milkweed had ever been inside the hollow tree, he wasn't any more, Fawn decided. She headed towards the opening.

Sunshine flooded her eyes. Fawn stopped, blinking in surprise at the strange landscape before her.

A sea of green grass stretched below her feet. But what odd grass! Every blade had been snipped off at the exact same height. Fawn flew down closer to examine the grass, trying to imagine what creature could have cut it just so. *Why,* she thought, *even the most talented harvest fairies couldn't have been so precise!*

And the flowers! Fawn stared in amazement. They grew in tidy rows, lined up as neatly as marching ants. Flowers in Pixie Hollow grew hither and thither, wherever the wind – or the garden fairies – planted them.

"What is this place?" Fawn murmured.

Then Fawn saw something that made her catch her breath.

Ahead, a massive structure rose up from the grass, so high it seemed to touch the sky. Fawn could tell from the doors and windows that the thing was a house. But who would live in such a place? It was bigger than the entire Home Tree!

Big enough to hold a whole *family* of Clumsies....

With a start, Fawn realized that she was looking at a Clumsy house. "But that's impossible!" she said aloud. Clumsies lived on the mainland, a place far, far from Pixie Hollow. So what was a Clumsy house doing inside an old fig tree?

Fawn knew she should fly straight back to the Home Tree and tell the queen what she'd found. But her curiosity got the better of her. Instead of going back, Fawn flew forward.

Right away, Fawn could tell she was no longer in Pixie Hollow. The air felt different. It *smelled* different. She could hear birds singing, but she didn't recognize their songs. Fawn heard other noises, too – strange rumbling sounds that came and went like sea waves. For the life of her, she couldn't have said what made them.

Fawn flew slowly through the flowers, enjoying the adventure. *What kind of animals live here?* she wondered. In Fawn's opinion, you couldn't know much about a place until you met its animals.

The house loomed in front of her. Flying up to a window, Fawn peeked inside. She saw what looked like a sitting room. There were chairs, lamps and a table. Books and shoes were scattered everywhere. But she didn't see any Clumsies.

Somewhere nearby, a bell jingled faintly.

"Milkweed?" Fawn called. She looked behind her, but the mouse didn't show a whisker.

There's something funny about that jingle, Fawn thought with a frown. Whatever was wearing the bell didn't move like a mouse.

Fawn spun round just in time to see something lunge towards her. She screamed. As she leaped from the windowsill, she caught a glimpse of yellow eyes and needle-sharp teeth.

Fawn zigzagged back the way she'd come, searching for the hollow fig tree. But each way she turned, she saw only a tall wooden fence. "Where is it?" she wailed, lurching this way and that. *"Where is it?"*

With a cold jolt of fear, Fawn realized that the tree wasn't there. The passage back to Pixie Hollow was gone!

Fawn glanced back over her shoulder. She saw now that her pursuer was a cat. His brown fur was striped like a tiger's, and his eyes were like amber. They narrowed as he stalked towards Fawn, his tail twitching eagerly.

Fawn gave up looking for the fig tree and searched for any escape. Along one side of the fence, she noticed a narrow gap between the wooden slats. It would be a tight squeeze. But it was her only chance.

Fawn raced towards the gap in the fence. She reached it just as the cat leaped. Fawn wriggled and twisted, trying to squeeze her wings through. She felt one of the boards move slightly, as though it was loose, and at last she shot through the gap. Behind her, the cat slammed against the fence with an angry yowl.

Fawn looked up and gasped. She was back in Pixie Hollow!

"Wh-what … but … how…?" Fawn stuttered. She spun around. She was hovering in front of the hollow fig tree.

Fawn's wings felt like they were going to give out. She sank to the ground, trembling all over. *It doesn't matter how I got here,* she thought. *The important thing is that I'm still alive.*

Fawn glanced back at the hollow tree and shivered. The tree was dangerous. She knew she had better tell Queen Clarion about it right away.

But as Fawn got up to leave, she heard a faint jingle. She looked back at the hollow. Two yellow eyes peered at her from the darkness.

"Oh, no!" Fawn cried as a blur of brown fur streaked towards her. She'd led the cat to Pixie Hollow!

chapter 4

Lainey trudged down the pavement
in a haze of disappointment. She,
Kate, Gabby and Mia had searched
all over Mia's back garden for the lost
bag of fairy dust. They'd combed the
flower bed, peeked under the patio
furniture and crawled on their knees
over the grass. They would have gone
on searching, too, if Mia's mother
hadn't said it was getting late and sent
them home.

Lainey's house was just three doors
down from Mia's, along a street lined

with tall, narrow homes and spindly trees. Lainey was so used to the path that she hardly noticed where her feet were taking her.

A ferocious bark startled her out of her thoughts. Lainey jumped back as a black-and-white dog threw itself against the fence she was passing.

Lainey saw this dog every time she visited Mia's house. Although Lainey loved all animals, she'd always been careful to steer clear of this one. The dog never stopped barking.

But maybe now she didn't need to be afraid. After all, she'd learned so much from Fawn. She'd befriended all kinds of animals in Never Land. Maybe she could make friends with this dog, too. *Someone with real animal talent could,* Lainey thought.

And hadn't Fawn told her she had animal talent?

Lainey took a step towards the fence. "There, there," she said soothingly. She didn't know how to speak Dog. But she mimicked the tone Fawn used when she was talking to an upset animal. "Don't be so grouchy. I'm your friend."

The dog paused mid-bark. It stood with its nose against the fence, watching her. "Good dog," Lainey said.

Then the dog began to bark again, louder than ever. Lainey turned and ran the rest of the way to her house.

As soon as she saw her front door, a wave of homesickness washed over her. Lainey took the steps two at a time and burst inside, crying, "I'm back! I'm back!"

"I'm in here, Lainey!" her mother called.

Lainey followed the sound of her voice to the kitchen. Her mother was standing with her back to the door, staring up at an open cupboard.

Tears sprang to Lainey's eyes. How long had it been since she'd seen her mother? Days? *Weeks?* Only now did Lainey realize how much she'd missed her parents while she was in Never Land. She hurried over to her mum and wrapped her arms round her waist.

"Hi, baby," her mum said distractedly. "How does spaghetti sound for dinner?"

"Spaghetti sounds good." Pushing her glasses up on her nose, Lainey straightened and turned to face her mother.

So much had happened to her in Never Land. Lainey felt different – no, she *was* different. She was sure her mother would see it in her face.

But, at that moment, Mrs Winters was busy searching the cupboard. She moved some tins around, muttering, "I was sure we had tomato sauce...."

Lainey tugged her mother's sleeve. "Mum ... "

"Yes, Lainey?" her mother asked, without looking down.

"Do you notice anything *different* about me?" asked Lainey.

At last her mother turned. "Oh, honey," she said with a sigh. "When was the last time you combed your hair? You look like you've been living in the jungle!" She ran her fingernails through Lainey's fine blonde locks.

"Go and run a brush through it, then call your dad and ask him to pick up some dinner on the way home from work. It looks like we'll have to have a takeaway again. We're out of spaghetti sauce."

"Okay," Lainey mumbled, crestfallen. Her throat ached, but this time it wasn't from homesickness. Suddenly, she was painfully aware of everything she'd lost – the doe and the dairy mice and her friendship with Fawn, the fairies and flamingos, the beauty of Never Land and the specialness she'd felt when she was there. Was even that part gone? Now that she was home again, was she just plain old Lainey?

"Goodness, sweetie, don't be upset. We can have spaghetti *tomorrow* night, if you really want," her mother said, misunderstanding.

Lainey sighed heavily and turned to leave. As she did, her gaze fell on something scuttling across the floor. It was a little grey mouse. Lainey stared. She'd never seen a mouse in her house before. A tiny jingling sound seemed to be coming from it. Looking closer, Lainey saw a bell hanging round its neck.

It was one of the fairies' dairy mice!

At that moment, Lainey's mother saw the mouse, too. "Aaah! Get out!" she shrieked, stomping her foot.

"Don't hurt it!" Lainey exclaimed.

But her mother was already striding over to the broom cupboard. She grabbed a brush and began to chase the mouse around the kitchen.

"Mum, stop!" cried Lainey.

"I won't have mice in *my* house!" her mother declared, swiping at it with the broom. The mouse dodged the bristles one last time and disappeared through a crack in the wall.

"You almost killed it!" Lainey wailed.

"Mice are *pests*," her mother said. "They're *vermin* that carry diseases. For all we know, there could be a whole nest of them living behind the walls." She shuddered. "I think I have some mousetraps down in the basement. For heaven's sake, stay away from there," she added, as Lainey kneeled down to peek into the crack. "Who knows what kind of germs that thing has."

Her mother stomped off towards the basement. As soon as she was gone, Lainey got down on her hands and knees to look into the hole.

"*Eeee-eee*," she squeaked softly.

Nothing happened, so she squeaked again. She could see a pair of beady black eyes gleaming inside the hole. "It's okay," Lainey whispered. "I'm your friend."

The mouse wiggled its whiskers, but it wouldn't come closer.

What was going on? Was it possible she'd lost her animal talent when she'd left Never Land?

Then Lainey had a scarier thought. Maybe she'd never had any animal talent at all. Maybe Fawn had only said that to be nice.

Lainey felt worse than ever. But she knew she didn't have time to mope. Her mother would be back with the mousetrap at any moment. Lainey had to find a way to keep the mouse safe.

She went to the cupboard and found a plastic container with a lid. Then she took a block of cheese from the refrigerator and cut off a slice.

She put the piece of cheese in front of the mouse hole. Then she stepped back and waited.

A moment passed. Then a pink nose poked out of the hole, followed by a set of whiskers. Slowly, the mouse crept out, sniffing at the cheese.

Slam! Lainey dropped the container over it. Carefully, she slid the plastic lid under the edge, leaving a little opening for air. Now the mouse was trapped.

"I'm sorry, I'm sorry," Lainey whispered to the mouse as she hurried to her room. She could feel the little animal scrabbling against the side of the plastic container. She'd have to find

a better place for it, maybe a shoe box.
But Lainey still felt ashamed. She knew
no self-respecting animal talent would
ever trap a mouse like this. What would
Fawn think if she saw Lainey now?

Another, more important question
burned in Lainey's mind – what was a
mouse from Pixie Hollow doing *here*?

Chapter 5

Fawn dodged left, then right, trying to shake the cat. Her shoulders ached and her breath came in gasps. She didn't know how much longer she could keep flying. But no matter how she twisted and turned, the cat was always just behind her.

Ahead, Fawn saw a raspberry bush. She headed straight for it, darting into the branches with her last bit of strength.

Fawn peered out from between the leaves. She could see the cat watching her hiding spot with its yellow eyes. "Why are you bothering me?" Fawn called out in Cat. She hadn't talked to many cats before, but the language came to her naturally. Part of an animal fairy's magic was being able to speak to any creature.

The cat blinked. It was clear that he wasn't used to being questioned by his prey. "Come out where I can see you, shiny bird," he said.

Shiny bird? Fawn thought, confused. Then she understood. *He thinks I'm a bird! He's attracted to my glow.*

"I'm not a bird!" she yelled to the cat. "I'm a fairy!"

The cat blinked again. "Dragonfly?"

Was it possible this cat had never seen a fairy before? "Not a dragonfly. A fairy!" Fawn shouted.

"Flying thing?" the cat said. If he'd had shoulders, he would have shrugged.

Fawn realized she was getting nowhere talking to him. She had to find another way out of this mess.

Fawn plucked a raspberry from the bush. She weighed it in her palm, considering. A single fairy wasn't strong enough to fight a cat. But Fawn knew cats were proud animals. Maybe if she wounded his pride, he would go away.

Fawn threw the berry as hard as she could, hitting the cat squarely between the eyes. The cat jerked back, startled. He shook his head quickly. Then he lifted his chin and stalked away, as if he had important business elsewhere.

Fawn grinned as the cat broke into a run. Her plan was working!

But a second later, her smile faded. The cat wasn't running *away* from Fawn – he was running *towards* something.

Just beyond the edge of the woods, a mouse cart was passing through the meadow. The cart driver, a sparrow man named Dooley, was whistling to himself. He didn't see the cat creeping up behind him.

"Dooley!" Fawn shrieked. "Look out!"

Too late! The cat landed on the cart, and its load of walnuts spilled across the trail. The cart mice squealed and bolted, throwing Dooley from his seat.

Dooley tried to fly, but the cat caught him between his front paws. He batted him back and forth, toying with him as if he were a ball of wool.

"Leave him alone, you ratty tabby!"
Summoning her courage, Fawn flew
right up to the cat's nose and gave his
whiskers a yank.

The cat yowled in pain and leaped
back. Fawn took the moment to grab
Dooley's hand. She pulled him to safety
down a nearby mole hole.

"Are you all right?" Fawn asked.
The stunned sparrow man's glow
flickered like a firefly. But he didn't

have any scratches as far as Fawn
could tell.

"Wh-wh –" Dooley stuttered. "Wh-
where did that monster *come* from?"

Before Fawn could reply, they
heard squeals. Fawn peeked out of the
hole. The driverless mouse cart was
careening in circles as the terrified
mice ran this way and that.

"He's going to get the mice!"
Fawn cried.

But to her surprise, the cat bounded
right past the mouse cart. Something
else had caught his eye.

Ahead was the Home Tree,
sparkling with the hundreds of fairies
who weaved in and out of its branches,
going about their business.

Fawn gasped. What had she
done? In trying to drive the cat away,

she'd brought him to the heart of the fairies' world!

"Stay here. I'll send someone to help you with the mice," Fawn told Dooley. Then she raced off towards the Home Tree to warn the other fairies.

In the pebbled courtyard in front of the Home Tree's knothole door, a group of fairies sat enjoying a picnic. The cat headed for them, his tail twitching with pleasure.

"Fly!" Fawn screamed. "Fly away!" But she was too far away to be heard.

Wham! The cat pounced, landing in the middle of the picnic. Seashell plates and acorn teacups crashed to the ground. Cries of horror filled the courtyard. The cat danced on his hind legs, swiping happily at the fairies as they darted out of the way.

In an instant, the Home Tree was in chaos. The singing-talent fairies' songs turned to screams. A laundry-talent fairy dropped a whole line of washing, which sailed away on the breeze. Fairies and sparrow men crashed into each other as they tried to escape.

Fawn grabbed a blueberry from an overturned barrel and threw it at the cat. But the cat was too dazzled by the fairies to even notice. He slunk round the trunk, looking for one to catch.

Between the roots at the back of the Home Tree was the entrance to the kitchen. The doorway was just wide enough to fit a small melon – or a large cat. As Fawn reached the back of the tree, she saw the tip of the cat's fluffy tail disappear inside.

"Oh, no!" Fawn gasped. The kitchen fairies would be trapped!

But a second later, the cat came streaking back out. Right behind him were a band of red-faced kitchen fairies. Some hollered and banged on pots and pans. Others pelted the cat with peppercorns.

The cat fled.

"Good thing we were making pepper soup today," the baking-talent fairy Dulcie said when she caught Fawn's eye.

When the cat was a good distance away, he stopped running. He paced back and forth, casting sulky glances at the Home Tree.

"But it looks to me like we haven't seen the last of that cat," Dulcie added.

chapter 6

Lainey awoke to the sound of fairy laughter. *It's Prilla coming to wake us up!* she thought.

She opened her eyes, expecting to see sunlight dappling the branches of the willow-tree room. Instead, she found herself staring at a painted white ceiling.

Lainey sat up. She was in her own bed in her own room. There was no willow tree and no fairy coming to wake her. Only thin sunlight coming through blue curtains and the smell of her parents' coffee brewing – the same things she'd woken to her whole life.

And yet … she could still hear a tiny bell-like sound.

Lainey leaned over the side of her bed. There was the old shoe box she'd put on the floor the night before. Holding her breath, Lainey lifted the lid....

The little mouse stood up on his hind legs to greet her, the bell round his neck jingling faintly. Lainey smiled. *So it wasn't a dream after all*, she thought.

"Good morning, fella," she said softly. She held out her finger to the mouse, who sniffed it with interest. He seemed less afraid than he had been the day before.

Now, for the first time, Lainey noticed a notch in his ear.

She remembered that one of the dairy mice had an ear like that.

"Milkweed?" she asked. "Is that you?"

The mouse didn't seem to hear her. He sniffed around the shoe box, as if looking for a crumb. Lainey was glad to see that he'd eaten the pizza crust she'd left for him the night before.

"I'll bet you're hungry for breakfast," she said. "Coming right up."

Lainey carefully placed the lid back on the box. She pushed it under the bed so her mother wouldn't find it, then went downstairs to get something to eat.

In the kitchen, she found a note from her mother saying she'd gone to pick up a few things at the shop and that her dad had gone into work.

Lainey placed a slice of bread in the toaster. She had just poured herself a glass of orange juice when the phone rang.

Lainey picked up the phone.

It was Mia.

"Mia!" Lainey cried. "Guess what I found –"

"It's awful, Lainey!" Mia interrupted, her voice cracking. "I can't find him anywhere!"

"Can't find who?" asked Lainey, confused.

"Bingo! He's *missing!*" Tearfully, Mia explained that the cat hadn't been seen since the day before. "He didn't come when I called him. I even put out a bowl of tuna, but he didn't turn up. He *never* misses fish."

"Maybe he's out exploring," Lainey suggested.

"He never leaves the back garden," Mia sniffled. "I'm worried something has happened. Will you help me look for him?"

"I'll be right there," Lainey said.

When she'd hung up, Lainey took the toast out of the toaster. She wrote a quick note to her parents, then hurried upstairs. She fed pieces of toast to the mouse as she got dressed.

After she was done, Lainey took the mouse out of the shoe box and gently placed him in the pocket of her jumper. "Don't worry, little fella," she whispered. "I'll take care of you. I promise."

When Lainey got to Mia's house, Mia and Gabby were sitting on the front steps. Mia's eyes were rimmed with red, as if she'd been crying. Kate was there, too, looking as if she hadn't slept very well.

"I was up all night, looking for the Second Star to the Right," Kate told Lainey. "But I couldn't find it. The queen never told us what it was to the right *of*. Not that it matters anyway," she added, "since we lost the fairy dust."

"Guys," said Lainey, "something really weird happened last night. You aren't going to believe it." Reaching into her jumper pocket, she pulled out the little mouse.

Mia jumped back in surprise. "Why are you carrying a mouse around?" she asked Lainey.

"It's not just any mouse," Lainey replied. "It's Milkweed."

"Milkwhat?" asked Kate.

"His name is Milkweed," Lainey explained. "He's one of the fairies' mice."

Gabby stepped forward to pet the mouse. "Hello, Milkweed," she said, stroking his head with the tip of her finger.

"What's so important about him?" asked Kate.

"Well, that's the thing," said Lainey. "Don't you wonder how he got here?"

"You brought him in your pocket," Kate pointed out.

"But I *found* him in our kitchen last night," Lainey said. "Don't you think it's strange that a Never Land mouse turned up in my home?"

"Can we talk about this later?" Mia said impatiently. "Right now, we really need to find Bingo!"

The girls decided to split up to look for the cat. Mia and Gabby took one side of the street, while Lainey and Kate took the other. They walked up and down the neighbourhood, calling Bingo's name. But they didn't spot so much as a single paw print.

Finally, they returned to Mia and Gabby's house. When Mrs Vasquez saw how disappointed they looked, she poured them glasses of lemonade. The girls took their drinks into the back garden. A dark cloud had settled over the group.

"We're never going to find Bingo," Mia said despairingly.

"We're never going to get back to Never Land," added Kate.

Something in the corner of the garden caught Lainey's eye. "Mia," she said, "when did you get that?"

"Get what?" asked Mia.

"That plastic flamingo," Lainey said, pointing to the tall pink bird in the flower bed. At that moment, the  flamingo turned its head. It fixed them with a bright yellow eye. "*Awnk!*" it honked.

The girls screamed and jumped to their feet. Lemonade spilled everywhere.

"Mia?" Mrs Vasquez called from inside the house. "What's going on?"

"Nothing, Mami!" Mia yelled. She looked back at the flamingo.

It was perched on one foot in the middle of Mrs Vasquez's rosebushes. "What is a *flamingo* doing here?" she whispered.

"Maybe it escaped from the zoo?" Kate suggested.

"Maybe," said Lainey, her heart filling with hope, "it came from Never Land!"

The other girls turned to her. But before anyone could reply, they heard footsteps coming from inside the house. "Quick!" Mia whispered. "Hide it!"

"Hide it?" said Kate. "How? It's as tall as we are!"

"I have an idea!" said Lainey. "Kate, kneel down. You too, Mia. Hurry!"

When Mrs Vasquez stepped outside a moment later, Gabby was sitting on Mia's shoulders and Lainey was sitting on Kate's shoulders. They crowded together in the corner of the garden, blocking the flamingo from her view.

"What on earth are you all doing?" Mrs Vasquez asked.

"We're having chicken races!" Lainey said brightly as Kate staggered beneath her, trying to keep her balance.

"*Awnk!*" honked the flamingo behind them.

"*Bok!*" shouted Lainey. "It's part of the game. You have to say, '*Bok, bok!*'"

"*Bok! Bok! Bok!*" The girls all began to yell to cover up the flamingo's noises.

Mrs Vasquez frowned. "It looks dangerous. Can't you girls play something where you all keep your feet on the ground?" She turned towards the house, then paused and looked back. "And, girls, please don't play too close to the flower bed. Those are my prize roses!" She slid open the screen door and went inside.

"Oof!" Kate grunted as she fell to the grass, tipping Lainey off her shoulders. "You're a lot heavier than you look. Now, what were you saying?"

Lainey's heart was beating fast. "What if the flamingo is from Never Land?" she whispered to her friends.

"What would it be doing here?" asked Mia.

For the first time since they'd lost the fairy dust, Kate's face lit up. "The fairies must have sent him! I'll bet he's here to show us the way back to Never Land!"

At once the girls turned towards the bird. It looked back at them warily.

"Come on, Mr Bird. Tell us how to get back to Never Land," Kate coaxed.

"Look!" cried Gabby. "He's trying to get away!" The flamingo was spreading his wings, as if he were about to take to the air.

"Not so fast!" cried Kate. She lunged at the flamingo, which hopped just out of her reach. Kate began to chase him through the flower bed. Petals flew from the roses.

"Kate!" Mia wailed. "Watch out for Mami's flowers!"

Kate ignored her and dived into the middle of the petunias. She managed to grab the flamingo by the leg.

"I got him … *ow*!" Kate cried as the flamingo beat her about the head with his wings, trying to escape. "Quick! Someone find something to hold him!"

"I know how to catch him!" Gabby hurried to the back door and grabbed

a butterfly net that was leaning against the house. She ran towards Kate and the flamingo, waving it.

"Don't!" cried Lainey. "He's scared." The flamingo was flapping his wings, straining to get away. At last the bird managed to pull his foot from Kate's grip. He rose into the air, sailed a short distance and landed on the roof of Mia and Gabby's house.

The girls stared up at him. "Well," said Mia, "*now* what do we do?"

"*Awnk!*" said the flamingo.

Chapter 7

Silence had settled across Pixie Hollow. In the gardens, the spider-thread hammocks hung empty. On Havendish Stream, the fairies' leaf-boats bobbed forlornly on their anchors. Not a whisper of wings could be heard across the meadow. The only sound was the splash of the waterwheel as it turned in the stream for an empty mill.

Inside the Home Tree, fairies peeked from the windows. They were watching for the furry beast that had driven them all behind doors. Many fairies had gathered in the grand dining hall. The serving-talent fairies were passing out acorn cups full of blackberry tea to soothe everyone's jangled nerves.

As Fawn wandered through the dining hall, she heard snippets of talk among the fairies.

"I've never seen a monster like that in Pixie Hollow before...."

"Did you see it knock down the bridge?"

"We can't stay inside forever! We'll starve, you know...."

In a corner of the dining hall, a small group of fairies hovered around Dooley. His glow had returned, but he still wore a tragic look on his face. He clutched a teacup and a plate of poppy-seed cake as he told his story. "I swear on my wings, I was

inches from being eaten! My whole life *flashed* before my eyes. Mmm. This is very tasty cake. You know, I think another slice might help me get my strength back...."

Fawn felt terrible. She knew that this was all her fault. If she hadn't flown into the Clumsy garden, the cat never would have chased her back to Pixie Hollow.

And yet, Fawn still didn't understand what had happened. How had she got to the Clumsy garden to begin with?

Fawn spotted Queen Clarion standing before one of the tall dining-hall windows. The queen held a cup of tea in her hand, but she never raised it to her lips. She gazed outside with a puzzled expression. Fawn made her way over to her.

Queen Clarion turned her head. "Oh, Fawn. I was just thinking how strange this all is. Usually Never creatures are respectful of the fairy realm – even the hawks and snakes."

Fawn cleared her throat. "The thing is," she began, "the cat isn't from Never Land."

The queen raised her eyebrows. "Then where did it come from?"

"I, ah, I don't really know," Fawn admitted. She explained how she'd gone looking for Milkweed and stumbled upon a Clumsy's house inside an old fig tree.

"What Clumsy?" asked Queen Clarion. "Was it a pirate? Or one of Peter Pan's boys?"

Fawn shook her head. "I don't know. I never saw any Clumsies there. But it wasn't just a house. The grass was different and the flowers were different. It even had a different sky. It was a whole Clumsy world."

"But that's impossible," said the queen. "To get to the world of Clumsies, you'd have to fly across the sea!"

"I don't understand it, either," said Fawn. "But that's where I saw the cat. He started to chase me. When I tried to escape, I found myself right back in Pixie Hollow – and the cat was with me!"

The queen furrowed her brow. "It doesn't make sense."

Tinker Bell had been sitting nearby, tinkering with a thimble bucket.

Suddenly, she spoke up. "Maybe there's a hole."

The queen and Fawn both turned to her. "What do you mean?" asked Queen Clarion.

"Like a shortcut between Never Land and the mainland," said Tink. "Usually, they're far apart. They exist in separate realms. But if there was a hole…."

Tink took the cup of tea from Queen Clarion's hand and poured it into the bucket. Tea dribbled out of the bottom. "Things could fall through."

"If there was a hole, wouldn't we know about it?" asked Queen Clarion.

"It could be a pinprick hole," Tink said. "They're the sneakiest kind. You don't know about them until you spring a leak."

"A hole between Never Land and the mainland," the queen murmured, her frown deepening. "If it's true, all kinds of dangers could reach Pixie Hollow."

Tink nodded. "The cat might be the least of our troubles."

Fawn chewed her lip. She'd just thought of something. "If there's a hole, that means things can go both ways."

"What are you saying?" asked Tink.

"If the cat followed me here, that means he can follow me back." Fawn lifted her chin bravely. "I'll lead

the cat back to the Clumsy house.
I'll use myself as bait."

The queen looked shocked. "I forbid
it," she said. "It's too dangerous."

"It's the only way," Fawn said. "If I
don't, we may be stuck inside the
Home Tree forever."

Tink stood up. "You can't do it alone.
I'll help you."

Fawn was about to say no. But when
she saw the fierce look in Tink's
eyes, she nodded. She would need all
the help she could get.

Chapter 8

"Somebody *do* something!" Mia said.

Kate took off her trainer and hurled it at the flamingo. The shoe sailed through the air, missing the bird by a mile. It landed in the gutter.

The flamingo looked at it curiously. It stepped over to the trainer and began to peck at the laces.

"That's just great," Kate groaned. She threw herself down on the grass. "Now a flamingo is eating my shoe."

"And I still don't know where Bingo is," Mia said, sinking down next to her. "This has got to be the worst day ever."

Lainey and Gabby sat down, too. Lainey took Milkweed from her pocket and stroked his furry head. *I wish I could talk to you*, she thought. *You could tell me what's going on.*

Suddenly, Milkweed twisted in her hands and leaped on to the grass. Before Lainey could grab him, he dashed across the lawn, wriggled through a narrow gap in the fence, and disappeared.

"Oh, no!" Lainey jumped up and ran to the fence. She tried to peer between the slats. "Where did he go?"

Gabby put her eye right up to the fence slats. "I see him!" she cried.

"Quick! Kate, Mia, give me a boost!" Lainey cried. Kate and Mia ran over and lifted Lainey so she could see over the top of the fence. Lainey scanned the neighbour's garden on the other side, but there was no sign of the mouse. "He's gone!"

"But I saw him. I did!" Gabby insisted.

"Well, he's gone now," Lainey said sadly as Mia and Kate helped her down.

Lainey imagined Milkweed loose in the alley. *What if he meets up with a cat or a dog or a mousetrap?* she thought. Even if he escaped those dangers, how would he find food or a safe place to sleep? Their city street was nothing like the mossy hammocks and flower-filled meadows of Pixie Hollow.

Why had he run away like that? All Lainey wanted to do was take care of him, but it seemed she'd failed even in that. She felt a lump in her throat.

She couldn't even look after a *mouse*!

How disappointed Fawn would be if she knew.

"Look, he's coming back!" Gabby said.

For one hopeful moment, Lainey thought she meant Milkweed.

But Gabby was pointing at the house. The girls watched as the flamingo lifted off from the roof. He glided down and landed on the grass, not far away from Lainey.

"*Awnk!*" The flamingo turned his head to one side. His beady eye stared at Lainey.

He looks like he wants to tell me something, she thought.

"It's no use," Lainey told the bird bitterly. "I don't understand."

"*Awnk!*" The flamingo took a few steps towards the fence, then twisted his neck to look back at Lainey. He reminded Lainey of the Never doe. Whenever she'd wanted to go for a run in the forest, she'd given Lainey a look like that, and Lainey had always understood.

But that was in Never Land, Lainey reminded herself. Here she didn't have animal talent. Still, she couldn't shake the idea that the flamingo was trying to tell her something.

"What is it?" Lainey whispered. She took a step towards the bird. Tentatively, she reached out and touched the flamingo's wing. His feathers felt silky beneath her fingers.

Suddenly, a net swooped down over the flamingo's head. Lainey looked up, startled, and saw Kate gripping the handle of the butterfly net.

"I got him!" Kate cried. "Now he can't get away!"

"Kate, stop! You're scaring him!" Lainey cried as the flamingo began to flail and whip his head.

"*Awnk! Awnk! Awnk!*" Lainey didn't need to have animal talent to know that the bird was upset. She grabbed the net from Kate's hands to set him free.

But at that moment, the flamingo began to run. For such a spindly bird, he was surprisingly strong. Still holding the butterfly net, Lainey was pulled along with it.

"Lainey, let go!" her friends yelled as the bird circled, dragging Lainey behind him.

"I can't!" Lainey cried. The butterfly net seemed to be attached to her arm. She looked down and saw a tiny wire loop on the handle. It had become hooked on to her lasso bracelet.

Then the flamingo quickly swung round and headed straight for the fence. "Stop! Stop!" Lainey screamed. But the bird charged towards the fence at full speed.

They were going to crash!

chapter 9

"Ready?" asked Fawn.

Tinker Bell checked the catapult on her belt, then nodded. "Ready."

That afternoon, Tink and Fawn had carefully made a plan to lure the cat back through the hole to the mainland. Fawn would go first, taunting the cat and leading him towards the hollow tree. Tink would follow her and act as lookout. Queen Clarion had given them both extra fairy dust to help them fly faster.

At the last moment, Tink had tucked the catapult and a pouch full of peppercorns into her belt. "Just in case," she'd told Fawn.

Fawn eased open the knothole door of the Home Tree and peeked outside. She could see the cat prowling around the roots of the tree.

Fawn took a deep breath. "Hey, fish breath!" she called out in Cat. The cat turned to look. Its eyes lit up at the sight of the fairy.

"Catch me if you can!" cried Fawn, and dived into the air.

The cat leaped after her. To make sure she had him hooked, Fawn led him on a winding chase through Pixie Hollow. First she flew towards the dairy barn. The cat followed closely, as she'd hoped he would.

Just before she reached the barn, Fawn made a hair clip turn and flew in the opposite direction, towards the fairy circle. Glancing over her shoulder, she saw the cat right behind her. His golden eyes were bright with pleasure, as if he were enjoying every moment of the chase.

"Nasty beast," Fawn muttered under her breath. "Only a monster wants to *play* with his lunch before he eats it."

She flew two loops round a hawthorn tree, making sure the cat stayed with her.

"You've got him!" Tink cried from somewhere to her left. "Now go!"

Fawn looped back round and headed towards Havendish Stream and the fairy-dust mill. She knew that just beyond, on the far side of the stream, was the hollow fig tree.

"Almost there," Fawn told herself. Soon this whole nightmare would be over. She put on a burst of speed.

But as the tree came into view, Fawn saw something sitting at the mouth of the hollow. As she drew closer, she realized who it was. "Milkweed!"

Hearing his name, the mouse looked up. He wiggled his whiskers in greeting.

Oh, no! thought Fawn. If she led the cat to the hollow now, he might go after Milkweed instead. Fawn didn't want to put the mouse in danger. But she couldn't keep going much longer. For a second, Fawn paused in the air, unsure what to do.

The moment's hesitation was all it took. The cat saw its chance and pounced.

"Fawn!" Tink screamed. "Look out!"

Fawn tried to lurch out of the way, but she was a second too late. The cat's paw struck her. It sent her spinning through the air.

Fawn plummeted towards the ground. She landed in Havendish Stream. Right away, Fawn knew she was in deep trouble. Like all Never fairies, Fawn couldn't swim. The second she hit the stream, her wings began to soak up water. They started to drag her down.

Just as Fawn's head was about to go under, she felt someone grasp her hand. Tink was trying to pull her out!

Tink fluttered her wings with all her might. As she did, her catapult

came loose from her belt. It landed with a splash next to Fawn and sank below the waves.

With her soaked wings, Fawn was too heavy to lift out of the stream. Still gripping Fawn's hand, Tink started to tow her through the water towards shore. At last, she managed to pull her on to the bank.

A shadow fell over them. The fairies looked up and saw the cat closing in.

"Fly!" screamed Tink. Fawn tried to flap her wings, but they felt like sandbags on her back.

The cat loomed over them. The last thing Fawn saw was the cat's lips peeling back from its needle-like teeth.

Fawn closed her eyes. As she braced herself, she heard a booming *"Awnk!"*

Her eyes flew open just in time to see a flamingo burst from the hollow tree. And dragging along behind it was ...

"Lainey!" Fawn cried.

If Lainey heard her, Fawn couldn't tell. The girl's eyes were squeezed tightly shut. Her hair was flying in every direction and her glasses hung from one ear. She clutched the handle of a large net, clinging to it as if for dear life.

Chapter 10

"Help!" Lainey cried.

The cat caught one glimpse of the flamingo and turned tail. It sprinted away, yowling in terror.

Suddenly, Lainey felt the flamingo come to a stop. She slowly peeled open one eye, then the other. She was back in Pixie Hollow!

"Awnk! Awnk!" Lainey heard another flamingo. She looked around but couldn't see it. Then she spotted Fawn. The fairy was calling to the bird in its

own language, calming it down.

But how did I get here? Lainey wondered. She looked behind her and saw Kate, Mia and Gabby climbing out of a hollow tree.

"It's you!" Tinker Bell cried when she saw the girls. "What are you doing here?"

"I don't know!" said Kate, looking equally surprised. "We were in Mia's back garden a second ago. We saw the flamingo pull Lainey through the fence, so we ran to help her –"

"And we ended up here!" Mia broke in. "How did we do that?"

It took a few moments for Fawn, Tink and the four girls to piece together what had happened. When the flamingo had dragged Lainey towards the fence, the girls had all thought they were going to crash.

"But instead, when they hit the fence, the slat swung sideways and they went right through," said Mia. "So we all followed Lainey, and here we are!"

"There's a loose board," Kate explained.

"And when you go through, you get to Never Land!" Gabby chimed in, not wanting to be left out of the story.

"I still don't understand," said Fawn. "How did you go from the broken fence to the hollow tree?"

Tink tugged her fringe, deep in thought. "The pinprick hole," she said at last.

"The what?" asked Lainey.

Tink explained her theory about the hole between Never Land and the mainland.

"So you mean there's a passage that goes from Pixie Hollow right to Mia and Gabby's back garden?" Kate exclaimed. "That's perfect! Now we can come back whenever we want!"

"It's not perfect," Tink said, her face serious. "In fact, it's very dangerous. We've already had problems. A cat has been on the loose in Pixie Hollow...."

"Did you say a *cat*?" Mia asked.

At that moment, they heard a bell jingling. The sound made Fawn's blood run cold. With a gasp, she turned and saw the cat running towards them.

"Fly, Tink!" Fawn cried. "Don't worry about me! Save yourself!"

But this time the cat barely seemed to notice the fairies. It ran right past Fawn – and straight into Mia's open arms.

"Oh, Bingo! I was so worried about you!" Mia said, rubbing her face in the cat's fluffy fur.

"You … *know* this cat?" Fawn asked.

"He's my Bingo," Mia replied, squeezing the cat tightly. "I've been looking all over for him. I was afraid he'd got into trouble."

"*Causing* trouble is more like it," Tink said. "He's frightened every fairy in Pixie Hollow. They're all cowering in the Home Tree at this very moment."

Mia lifted Bingo up so they were nose to nose. "Bingo! Bad boy!" she scolded.

Bingo only yawned in reply. "Don't let him fool you," Mia told the fairies. "He may pretend to be tough, but he wouldn't hurt a fly. He just wants to play."

"To play?" Fawn echoed faintly. "You mean, the cat has only been trying to play with us this whole time?"

Mia nodded. "I know he can be a bit rough, but it's not his fault. He's still just a baby – not much older than a kitten. He loves to have fun."

Tink rolled her eyes. "Some kind of fun."

The sound of another bell made everyone turn. A little grey mouse was making his way towards them.

"Milkweed!" Lainey cried in relief. She picked him up and watched the mouse sniff the palm of her hand. She knew she needed to tell Fawn the truth – that she didn't really have animal talent, after all. She wondered if Fawn would still want to be her friend.

"I lost Milkweed on the mainland,"

Lainey confessed to Fawn. "I thought I'd lost him for good. I couldn't communicate with him at all – or with the dog or any other animals. I don't really have animal talent," she added. "At home, I'm not really good at anything. I'm just a regular old Clumsy."

"Oh, Lainey," Fawn said. "Animal talent doesn't come and go. It's something in your heart. And you have a very big heart. That's even more important than being able to speak to animals. Speaking isn't everything – even I sometimes misunderstand," she added with a glance at Bingo.

"So you still want to be my friend?" Lainey asked.

"Of course," said Fawn. She was too tiny to hug Lainey, so she hugged her thumb instead.

Lainey felt better. "And now I can come and visit you any time!" she said. "All we have to do is go through the fence."

"What *are* you going to do about the hole?" Kate asked Tinker Bell. "You're not going to close it up, I hope?"

"I wouldn't even begin to know how," Tink replied. She tugged her fringe, thinking. "Still, the hole is dangerous. We have to do something. We'll start by telling Queen Clarion."

"Why don't you come with us?" Fawn said to the girls. "All the fairies are in the Home Tree right now. They'll be so glad to see you. Lainey, my wings are too wet to fly. Will you carry me?"

Together, the girls and the fairies set off for the Home Tree. Lainey was filled with pride carrying Fawn on her shoulder. There were so many questions still to be answered – about the hole in the fence that led to Never Land and whether she had animal talent. But one thing no longer bothered her. Lainey was certain now that she was special. For, she thought, there was nothing more special in the world than being a fairy's friend.

Don't miss the first magical book in the Never Girls series!

There it was. That sound again.

Kate McCrady froze. The football rolled past her, but she didn't even notice. She cocked her head to one side, listening.

Yes, it was the same sound she'd been hearing all afternoon. High and silvery, like little bells ringing. Kate looked around the back garden. What could it be?

"I got it!" yelled Lainey Winters. She chased the ball into the corner of the garden. Lainey's big glasses slid down her nose as she scooped up the ball. "I got it!" she cried again. "Kate's the monkey in the middle now!"

Across the lawn, Kate's best friend, Mia Vasquez, put her hands on her hips. "What's the matter, Kate?" she asked. It wasn't like Kate to miss such an easy pass.

"Do you hear that sound?" Kate asked her.

"What sound?" Mia replied.

"What's going on?" called Lainey, feeling left out. "Aren't we playing?"

Kate listened again. She couldn't hear the bells any more. She felt excited, although she didn't know why. "It was nothing, I guess," she said, turning back to the game.

"You're in the middle now," Mia reminded her.

Kate shrugged. She was good at football. She was good at most things that involved running, jumping, kicking or catching. She was never in the middle for very long.

"Okay, Lainey. You come and take my spot," she called. "Lainey! Lainey?"

*

Lainey didn't hear her. She was staring up at the sky. A flock of flamingos was passing overhead.

Flamingos? thought Lainey. *That can't be right.* Lainey's science book had a picture of a flamingo in it. Flamingos lived in warm, sunny places. They lived near seas and lakes. They didn't live in cities like Lainey's.

Maybe her glasses were playing tricks on her. Lainey took them off and rubbed them on her T-shirt. When she put them back on, the flamingos were gone. Where they'd been, Lainey saw only feathery clouds.

"Lainey!" Mia yelled.

Lainey looked over, startled. "Did you see the flamingos?" she asked.

From the way Kate and Mia stared at her, Lainey could tell she'd said something wrong. She felt her face turn red.

"We're ready to play," said Kate. "But you have the ball."

Lainey looked down at the ball in

her arms. "Oh, right." Lainey set the ball down on the grass. She glanced up at the sky one last time. Not a flamingo in sight.

But as the clouds drifted towards the horizon, Lainey could have sworn she heard the sound of flapping wings.